A GOLDEN BOOK • NEW YORK

The Animals' Christmas Eve copyright © 1977, copyright renewed 2005 by Random House, Inc.
Illustrations copyright © 2007 by Alex Steele Morgan.
The Christmas Story copyright © 1952, copyright renewed 1980 by Random House, Inc.
The Night Before Christmas copyright © 2001 by Random House, Inc.
All rights reserved. Published in the United States by Golden Books, an imprint of Random House Children's
Books, a division of Random House, Inc., 1745 Broadway, New York, NY 10019. *The Animals' Christmas Eve*
was originally published in slightly different form by Western Publishing Company, Inc., in 1977.
The Christmas Story was originally published in slightly different form by Simon and Schuster, Inc.,
and Artists and Writers Guild, Inc., in 1952. *The Night Before Christmas* was originally published by
Golden Books Publishing Company, Inc., in 2001. Golden Books, A Golden Book, A Little Golden Book,
the G colophon, and the distinctive gold spine are registered trademarks of Random House, Inc.
www.randomhouse.com/kids
Library of Congress Control Number: 2009921719
ISBN: 978-0-375-85778-2
PRINTED IN SINGAPORE
10 9 8 7 6 5
First Random House Edition 2009

The Animals' Christmas Eve

By Gale Wiersum • Illustrated by Alex Steele Morgan

In the barn on Christmas Eve,
After all the people leave,
The animals, in voices low,
Remember Christmas long ago.

One small hen, upon her nest,
Softly clucks to all the rest:
"Little chicks, come, gather near.
A wondrous story you will hear."

Two white doves, on rafters high,
Coo a quiet lullaby:
"Long ago in manger hay,
The little baby Jesus lay.

"Three wise men from far away
Came to visit him one day,
For he was born," the doves recall,
"To be the greatest king of all!"

Four brown horses in their stalls,
Snug within the stable walls,
Tell of his birth: "'Twas long foretold
By chosen men in days of old."

Five gray donkeys speak with pride,
Remembering one who gave a ride:

"Our brother donkey went with them
From Nazareth to Bethlehem."

Six spotted calves now nibble hay
Like that on which the baby lay.

"They put him in a manger bed
So he could rest his sleepy head."

Seven goats, all black and white,
Describe the sky that holy night:

"A star appeared at early morn
To mark the place where he was born."

Eight nestling kittens lick their fur.
They nod their heads and softly purr.

"And he was wrapped in swaddling clothes
To keep him warm from head to toes."

Nine woolly sheep, down from the hill,
On Christmas Eve remember still:

"Shepherds heard the angels sing
Praises to the newborn king."

Ten soft lambs say Jesus' name.
"He was the Lamb of God who came.

He was the greatest gift of love,
Sent from his Father, God, above."

Eleven puppies listen well,
In hopes that they, in turn, can tell

The Christmas story another year
For all the animals to hear.

Twelve chimes ring out from far away—
The lovely bells of Christmas Day.
And every beast bows low its head
For one small babe in a manger bed.

THE
CHRISTMAS STORY

By Jane Werner

Illustrated by
Eloise Wilkin

THIS IS MARY, a girl of Galilee.

She lived long years ago, but such a wonderful thing happened to her that we remember and love her still.

One day an angel appeared to Mary.

"You are blessed among women," the angel said, "for you shall have a son, whom you shall name Jesus. He shall be called the Son of God, and his kingdom shall never end."

"I am glad to serve the Lord," said Mary. "May it be as you have said."

Then the angel left her.

Mary married a good man from Nazareth. His name was Joseph, and he was a carpenter by trade.

When Joseph had to go from Nazareth up to
Bethlehem in Judea, to pay his taxes in his father's
town, Mary went with him. It was a long, weary
journey for her.

When they reached Bethlehem at last, they found
many travelers there before them. The streets were full
of cheerful, jostling kinsmen.

The inns were crowded to the doors.
Though Joseph asked shelter only for his wife,
every innkeeper turned them away.

At last one innkeeper, seeing Mary's weariness and
need, showed them to a stable full of warm, sweet hay.

There Mary brought forth her son. And she wrapped
him in swaddling clothes and laid him in the manger,
since there was no room for them in the inn.

THERE WERE IN that same country shepherds
in the field, keeping watch over their flocks by night.

An angel of the Lord appeared to them in shining glory, and they were all afraid.

UT THE ANGEL said to them:

"There is nothing to fear. I come to bring you news of great joy which shall come to all people.

"For a child is born this day in Bethlehem— a Saviour who is Christ the Lord.

"And this shall be a sign to you. You shall find the babe wrapped in swaddling clothes and lying in a manger."

Suddenly the sky was full of angels, praising God and saying, "Glory to God in the highest, and on earth peace, good will toward men."

When the angels disappeared into heaven, the shepherds said to one another, "Let us go to Bethlehem and see this thing which the Lord has made known to us."

They hurried to the town and found Mary and
Joseph, and the babe lying in the manger. Afterwards,
the shepherds told everyone they met about the child.

NOW WHEN JESUS was still a baby, three wise
men from the East came to Jerusalem. "Where is he that
is born King of the Jews?" they asked. "For we have seen
his star in the East, and are come to worship him."

When Herod the King heard this, he was troubled in his wicked heart. He called the wise men to him and asked them just when the star had appeared.

Then he sent them off to Bethlehem, saying, "Go and search for the young child, and when you have found him, bring word back to me, that I may come and worship him also."

When they had heard the king, the wise men departed. Behold, the star which they had seen in the East went before them, till it stood over the place where the child lay. When they saw the star, the wise men rejoiced and were glad.

And when they came into the house, they saw the
young child with Mary his mother, and bowed down and
worshiped him. They opened their treasures and laid before
him gifts: gold and frankincense and myrrh.

Being warned by God that they should not return to
Herod, they departed for their own country another way.

The child was called Jesus, the name given by
the angel before he was born. And the child grew
and became strong in spirit and full of wisdom.
And the grace of God was upon him.

The Night Before
Christmas

By Clement C. Moore

Illustrated by Mircea Catusanu

'Twas the night before Christmas,
when all through the house,

Not a creature was stirring, not even a mouse.
The stockings were hung by the chimney with care,
In hopes that St. Nicholas soon would be there.

The children were nestled all snug in their beds,
While visions of sugarplums danced in their heads.

And Mamma in her kerchief, and I in my cap,
Had just settled down for a long winter's nap
When out on the lawn there arose such a clatter,
I sprang from the bed to see what was the matter.

Away to the window I flew like a flash,
Tore open the shutters and threw up the sash.
The moon on the breast of the new-fallen snow
Gave the luster of midday to objects below,

When, what to my wondering eyes should appear,
But a miniature sleigh and eight tiny reindeer
With a little old driver so lively and quick,
I knew in a moment it must be St. Nick.

More rapid than eagles his coursers they came,
And he whistled, and shouted, and called them by name:
"Now, Dasher! Now, Dancer! Now, Prancer and Vixen!
On, Comet! On, Cupid! On, Donder and Blitzen!
To the top of the porch! To the top of the wall!
Now dash away! Dash away! Dash away all!"

As dry leaves that before the wild hurricane fly,
When they meet with an obstacle, mount to the sky,
So up to the housetop the coursers they flew,
With the sleigh full of toys, and St. Nicholas, too.

And then in a twinkling, I heard on the roof,
The prancing and pawing of each little hoof.

As I drew in my head, and was turning around,
Down the chimney St. Nicholas came with a bound.

He was dressed all in fur, from his head to his foot,
And his clothes were all tarnished with ashes and soot.
A bundle of toys he had flung on his back,
And he looked like a peddler just opening his pack.

His eyes, how they twinkled! His dimples, how merry!
His cheeks were like roses, his nose like a cherry!
His droll little mouth was drawn up like a bow,
And the beard on his chin was as white as the snow.

The stump of his pipe he held tight in his teeth,
And the smoke, it encircled his head like a wreath.
He had a broad face and a little round belly
That shook when he laughed, like a bowl full of jelly.

He was chubby and plump, a right jolly old elf,
And I laughed when I saw him, in spite of myself.

A wink of his eye and a twist of his head
Soon gave me to know I had nothing to dread.
He spoke not a word, but went straight to his work,
And filled all the stockings, then turned with a jerk.

And laying his finger aside of his nose,
And giving a nod, up the chimney he rose.

He sprang to his sleigh, to his team gave a whistle,
And away they all flew like the down of a thistle.
But I heard him exclaim, as he drove out of sight,

"Happy Christmas to all.

And to all a good night."